THE KNIGHT

By Big Red Chicken™ aka Lance Nevis

Illustrated by Tom Piper

THE KNIGHT

Written by Lance Nevis
aka Big Red Chicken ™

Illustrated
by
Tom Piper

Editor-in-Chief
Lance E. Nevis

Formatted for Publications
by
Tom Piper

Published
by
Animal Rain Productions Publishing Co.
Featuring Big Red Chicken ™

To contact Author, Illustrator, Editors or Publisher:
1630 Williams Hwy. #351 Grants Pass, Oregon 97527 / animalrainproductions@gmail.com

 Library of Congress cataloging in publication data: Lance Nevis, Fiction, Juvenile Literature. Summary : The life of a boy growing up and becoming a royal knight.

Library Of Congress Number: 2018959045
ISBN: 978-0-6921940-6-5

Printed in United States of America

Dedicated to Mikey

I would like to dedicate this book to my nephew Mike Jr. Mike Jr. continues to struggle with Autism each and every day. He has made tremendous progress and the best is yet to come. Mike Jr. has an incredible strong will! Whatever he sets his mind on, he will accomplish! It is such a joy to be a part of his life and watch him grow. Mike Jr. you are Dad's "Hero", your sister's "Squishy" & Best Friend and as your Mom loves to tell you every-day... "I'm so lucky you're mine!" These are my sentiments also. We are so lucky you are a part of our family. We love you Mike Jr. always and forever.

Love ,
Uncle Lance
Big Red Chicken ™

To learn more about Autism: www.autismspeaks.org

CHAPTER 1

The early years

I went to bed
and thought a good knight
with dreams in my mind
no matter the sight.

‘Cause I’ve been in battles
while I was asleep
with warriors and demons
being kept in the keep.

So dreaming and wanting
the Queen's accolade
I will slay me a dragon
by the time I awake.

The sun rises fast
and I pray my Lord
so I jump right up
and put on my sword.

100
90
80
70
60
ROYAL
THERMOMETER

I sweat in this heat
to perfect my story
with me being knighted
by the Queen and her glory.

CHAPTER 2

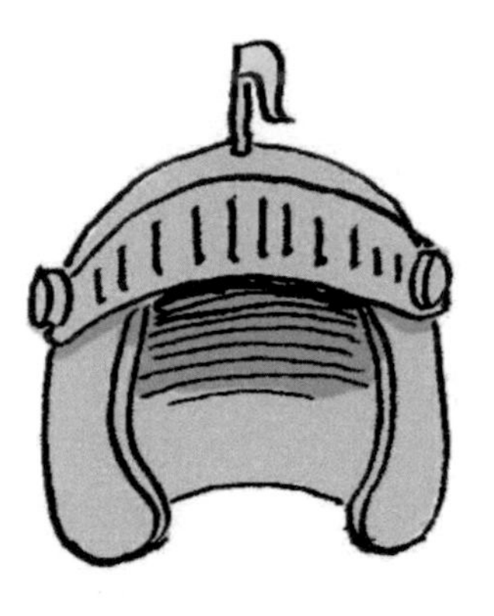

Midlife and becoming a knight

I fought in huge wars
and saw all the horrors of
plunder and suffer and
hate but these are the
things that hone a good
man into knighthood
and I couldn't wait.

And then the day came
the whole kingdom there,
with 88 soldiers
all kneeled in the square.

She went down the row
touched her sword to them all
now 87 knights
all standing up tall.

She then stopped at me
as my moment came
now knighted I stood
with fortune and fame.

CHAPTER
3

The later years of life

So then I grew older
and fought all my foes
and now all the kingdom
so the Queen also knows...

...if you're in your deepest
and darkest despair

just know the Knight
will always be there.

snore
snore

Like Lancelot back
in the times of old lore

when I go to bed
I hope I can snore...

...then wake up so proud
like I’ve always done

and live through my battles
with the help of the Son.

THE END

THE KNIGHT COLORING BOOK

Color your own pictures!

"Ah, it's so nice to dream."

“OK, if you keep wanting to fight...I’ll fight you.”

“Yes, I’ll do anything for you my Queen.”

"Well, it's time to get started."

"It sure is hot out here."

Many battles were fought.

And the big day comes.

"Thank you my Queen."

“Leave now and don’t come back.”

"I'll always be here to help you."

"Snore.....Snore..."

"Well, it's another beautiful day."

Big Red Chicken ™

About the Author

The author, Lance Nevis

Born in Sacramento in 1964, I have long dreamed of doing something to make a difference. I have always had an artistic side playing music, singing and writing my whole life. My hopes are that one day these books will help raise money and awareness towards the fight against autism. My first book was Animal Rain in 2007. I have since then started my own publishing company which is called Animal Rain Productions.

On a fishing trip three years ago a little boy was running up and down the shore insisting that I was Big Red Chicken TM . His Dad said, "Son, you don't know him well enough to call him that." The boy then said, "No Dad, that's Big Red Chicken TM ! " Since then it has stuck. So I hired an attorney and trademarked the name, Big Red Chicken TM and this is the symbol to go with it.

My books are made to bring people together and instill imagination. Although it has been a struggle getting noticed, I have endured and continue to believe in my dream that one day these stories will be in the hands of many and bring joy and a smile to them all!

Thank you for all the support that has ben given to me on this incredible journey.

God Bless,
Big Red Chicken TM
aka Lance Nevis

A special "Thanks" to my Mom and Dad who sometimes think I am a little crazy but yet continue to support me.

Made in the USA
San Bernardino, CA
10 November 2018